BILLY THE

KID

&

CROOKED

JIM

BILLY THE KID & CROOKED JIM

Hideout Kids Book 6

by
Mike Gleason

Illustrated by Victoria Taylor

FARM STREET PUBLISHING

First published 2018 by Farm Street Publishing
www.hideoutkidsbooks.com

Paperback ISBN 978-1-912207-15-2
Hardback ISBN 978-1-912207-16-9
eBook ISBN 978-1-912207-17-6

A CIP catalogue record for this book is available from
the British Library.

Design and typesetting by Head & Heart

To Michelle and Luke,
who inspired me to write these stories
of the Wild West.

TUFF

SADIE

CONTENTS

Dear Reader,

Billy the Kid & Crooked Jim is the sixth in the series of Hideout Kids books.

In the Wild West the most valuable land was known as "range land" or "ranges". The ranges were home to farms with crops and ranches with thousands of cattle. Battles were fought between honest ranchers and farmers and outlaws who wanted to steal the land and the cattle. These battles were known as "range wars".

The biggest range war of all was The Lincoln County War, fought in the Territory of New Mexico, near Muleshoe, the home of the hideout kids.

Judge June sends Tuff and Sawbones on a dangerous journey to Lincoln County to help an honest rancher battle the outlaws.

If you want to curl up with a good story, start curling and turn the page.

Mike Gleason

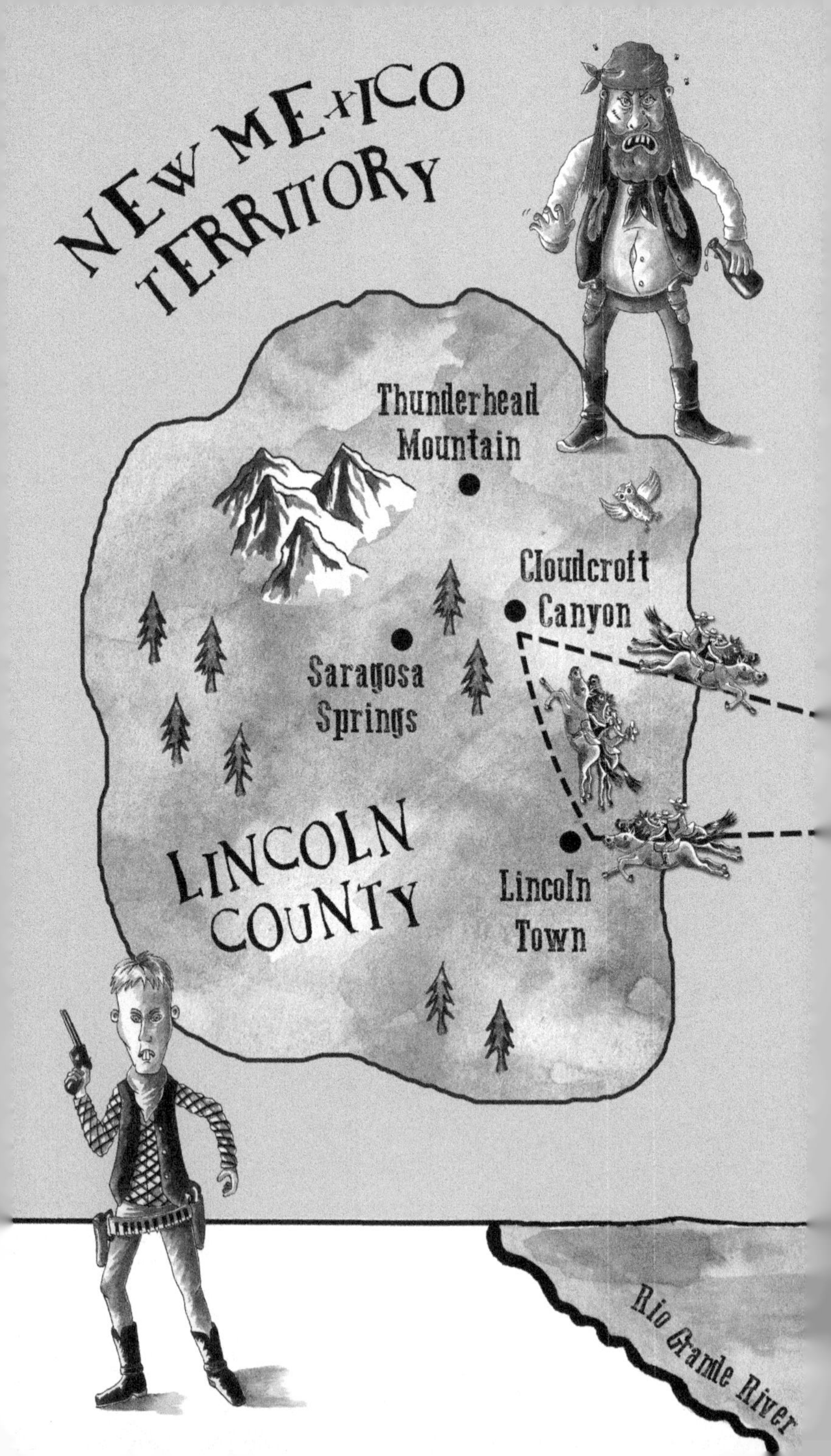

NEW MExICO TERRITORY

Thunderhead Mountain

Cloudcroft Canyon

Saragosa Springs

LINCOLN COUNTY

Lincoln Town

Rio Grande River

TUFF AND SAWBONES'
RIDE TO THE
LINCOLN COUNTY WAR

Canadian River

• Muleshoe

TE X AS

Pecos River

BILLY THE KID

KID

&

CROOKED

JIM

CHAPTER ONE

A LIGHTNING STRIKE

Late one spring afternoon dark storm clouds gathered above the Wild West Texas town of Muleshoe. Gusts of wind threw old leaves and tiny dung beetles through the air.

Whirling clouds of dust, which the hideout kids called "dust devils", danced around the town. Thunder rolled off the hills.

"We better duck for cover," Sheriff Tuff Brunson said as he walked up Main Street with his two deputies. "Here comes a nasty thunderstorm."

Tuff's deputies, Sadie Marcus and Joe "Sawbones" Newton, held on to their white hats and hurried into the Happy Days Saloon. "See you in a minute," Tuff shouted. "I'll make sure the jailhouse is secure."

Tuff ran to the wooden jailhouse. Locked up inside was The Parrot Gang, "Big Nose" George Parrot, the meanest outlaw in the West, his brother "Little Nose" George and sister "Tiny Nose" Peggy.

As the thunder boomed Big Nose George whimpered in a corner. Little Nose George was tucked under his arm, tears streaming down his cheeks.

"What's the matter, pretty Parrots?" Tuff laughed. "Scared of a little storm?"

"He's afraid of lightnin' and thunder, Sheriff," Little Nose George said. "Me too. Lightnin' might strike us. Even our horses are scared."

The jailhouse had a stables cell where Tuff locked up the outlaws' naughty horses.

"We're terrified," the horses whinnied.

"Your sister doesn't look scared," Tuff said. Tiny Nose Peggy stood by a window, grinning at the sky. Her arm stuck out between the metal bars.

Little Nose George stared at her. "Yeah, well, she's only thirteen. She don't know bad things can happen in a thunderstorm."

Tuff said, "Just relax. Your teenage brain is imagin—"

"BOOM! BOOM!"

A bright lightning flash set off a huge explosion of thunder.

Tuff was blinded. His ears rang and he fell to the floor. His head spun round and round...

"Tuff, Tuff, wake up," Sadie shouted. "C'mon Tuff, please wake up." She splashed his face with cold water.

Tuff sat up slowly, rubbing his eyes. He looked at Sadie. Sawbones stood next to her.

"What the —?" he gasped. "What happened to me?"

"Lightning struck the jailhouse," said Sawbones. "Sadie and I saw it from the doors of the saloon. Let me have a look at you." Sawbones was a doctor.

He examined Tuff carefully. "You should be OK. We need to keep one eye on you though."

"That won't be hard for you." Tuff giggled. Sawbones only had one eye. He lost his right eye in a fight.

"That's a good

sign," said Sawbones. "You've still got your sense of humor."

Tuff looked over at the cells. "Big Nose George. The Parrot Gang. They're gone."

CHAPTER TWO

WILD THING EATS A PARROT

"Sheriff, Sheriff," came a weak cry. "We're over here."

"What's that noise?" Tuff said. "It sounds like baby chicks chirping."

"Oh, look," Sadie said. She pointed at the rough wood floor of the wrecked jail. "I can't believe what happened. The lightning shrunk the Parrots."

"Let me have a look," Tuff said as he stood up and joined Sadie. The three Parrots and their three horses ran around in circles by her foot. "Oh dear, they're miniature."

He heard the sound of dinky hooves and the scuffle of tiny boots. "Now *that* is funny." He laughed. "They're really parrot-size now. I must be dreaming."

"It's not a dream," said the voice of Judge Junia "June" Beak. She appeared in the doorway. "This type of thing can happen to people who behave very badly. There is always a price to pay for bad behavior."

Wild Thing, Judge June's pet pink fairy armadillo, ran into the jail. "Oh, look at those yummy little birdies. I'm gonna eat 'em right up." She licked her chops. "Here I come."

She chased the Parrots and their tiny horses around the jail while the kids laughed.

"Please help us Judge June," squeaked teeny Tiny Nose Peggy. "We didn't mean to be mean. Your ugly armadillo is gonna eat us."

"Don't call me ugly," Wild Thing growled. "CHOMP!"

"Ow," squealed the girl bandit.

Judge June reached down and grabbed Tiny Nose Peggy from Wild Thing's jaws.

"You rescued her but you can't save this little parrot," Wild Thing shouted as she got Little Nose George in her mouth.

She swallowed the miniature Parrot.

"Good going, Wild Thing," Big Nose George said. "I'm finally rid of my smelly little brother."

"Wait, I feel sick now." Wild Thing started to turn purple.

She threw up Little Nose George who splattered over his older brother's head, covering him in armadillo vomit.

"That's just enough," Judge June said as she grabbed Wild Thing and tossed her over to the side of the jail.

Little Nose George slithered over his brother's back and lay crumpled on the floor.

Judge June held up an empty burlap sack. She dropped Tiny Nose Peggy inside.

"Deputies, put the
Parrot brothers and
their horses in this
sack," she ordered. "I'll
deal with them later. Tell
Deputy Dan to get this
jailhouse repaired."

Sawbones went to get Deputy Dan while
Tuff and Sadie scooped up the little Parrot
brothers.

"Yuck," Sadie said as she picked up Little

Nose George. Armadillo vomit dripped from his tiny boots.

"Ouch, be careful," peeped Little Nose George. "That mean Wild Thing almost turned me into armadillo poop."

Sadie dropped him in the burlap sack with his brother and sister just as Sawbones walked back in with Deputy Dan.

Judge June said, "Tuff, I need you to speak to you, Sadie and Sawbones. I have an urgent job for you. There is big trouble afoot."

"Bye-bye, birdies," Tuff said as he twisted the sack closed and tied it tightly. He turned to his jailhouse assistant. "Here, Deputy Dan. Hang this in a cell once you've got the jail cleaned up. Watch that sack."

"I'll guard the sack," Wild Thing growled, licking her chops.

"No you won't; you just threw up," Judge June said. "Come with us."

The afternoon sun shone brightly after the storm. The cool spring air smelled clean as they hurried across Muleshoe's Main Street.

Mr. Zip came over from his lodge in the stream that ran through the town. "Bad storm, huh?" he said as he joined them. "Were you scared, Wild Thingy?"

"Oh shut up, Mr. Blip," Wild Thing said. "You know I'm not afraid of a little thunder. You probably hid in your dam."

Judge June opened the bright yellow door leading into her two-story wooden hut.

Tuff felt the hut's cool air as the door closed behind them. A black bear with massive claws and bared teeth stood in one corner of the room.

"Still think he's dead and stuffed?" Sadie whispered. "Every time I see him he moves a claw."

Tuff shuddered.

Detailed maps hung on the walls and there were piles of books everywhere. Laid out across Judge June's desk was a map on yellow parchment.

A circle drawn in bright red paint curved around its center:

Lincoln County, Territory of New Mexico

On the edge of the map another circle was drawn around their town:

Muleshoe, State of Texas

"Lincoln County," Tuff exclaimed. "Home of The Lincoln County War. It's right next to us."

"You're right," Judge June said. "Lincoln County is where they're fighting the deadliest range war ever fought in the Wild West. The new Governor of New Mexico Territory, Army General Lew Wallace, has to stop it. He's under direct orders from the President of the United States."

"Who started the war?" Sadie asked.

"The Nasty Boys, a gang of vicious outlaws

led by 'Crooked' Jim Murphy," Judge June answered. "He wants to take over Lincoln County and steal everything. The Nasty Boys are fighting against an honest rancher named Sheriff John Robin. He formed a posse called The Bobbies."

"It's The Nasty Boys versus The Bobbies," growled Wild Thing. "Not as fun as Wild Thing versus Mr. Zip, is it, you stinky beaver?"

"Be quiet, Wild Thing," Judge June scolded. She continued, "Sheriff Robin and The Bobbies were outnumbered and went into hiding. General Wallace asked for my help so I sent my familiar, the owl Hooter, to find them. Now that we know where they are General Wallace has sent US Army soldiers from Camp Beak to guard them."

"Camp Beak is near Muleshoe," Sadie said. "The troops can get there quickly."

"Not quickly enough," Judge June said. "They need a bit more time. General Wallace asked me to send someone over to slow

down The Nasty Boys while they hunt for
The Bobbies. I told him I would send Tuff
and Sawbones. Sadie, I need you to stay here
for now."

"Good," Tuff said as he clenched his teeth.
"We can handle this job."

But can we? he wondered. *Sawbones and me
against an outlaw army?*

CHAPTER THREE

TUFF HATCHES A PLAN

"I thought so," said Judge June. "This job is extremely dangerous. You have your bullwhip, Tuff. Sawbones, take this."

Judge June handed Sawbones a beautiful pearl-handled leather bullwhip.

"We're a two-kid army," said Sawbones as he admired his whip.

Maybe you think so, Tuff thought. *I hope we're not a two-kid meal for The Nasty Boys.*

"Hooter will tell you what he found out

when he flew over to New Mexico. He's waiting for you in the jailhouse," Judge June said. "Also The Bobbies are very dangerous. Sheriff Robin hired some of the fastest gunfighters in the West, including the very fastest."

"Who's that?" Tuff asked.

"Billy the Kid."

"Whoa," said Tuff and Sawbones as they let out a breath.

Judge June said, "Now close your eyes very tightly."

Tuff, Sawbones and Sadie all closed their eyes. Judge June raised her arms to the sky. She murmured a spell.

A cool breeze filled the hut.

"You may open your eyes now," she said. "Be afraid of nothing."

The good witch Judge June looked at them with her magical, almond-shaped, blue-gray eyes. "Remember, now more than ever, my advice to you. It's easier to *stay* out of trouble than *get* out of trouble. Please be very careful."

Tuff, Sadie and Sawbones hustled across to the jailhouse. "Hello, law officers," Hooter said as they strolled in.

"Wow, look at this," Tuff exclaimed.

The jailhouse was completely rebuilt, exactly as it was before the lightning strike.

"I had a few minutes free so I decided to fix it," Hooter explained. "I'm sure Deputy Dan would have helped had he been awake." Deputy Dan snored from his rocking chair.

"GET UP!" Tuff ordered, right in Deputy Dan's ear. The deputy stumbled to attention, arms flapping.

"Is it suppertime?" he asked.

"No. Deputy Dan, you need to be more useful. Where's that sack full of little Parrots?"

"Don't worry," Hooter smiled. "They're hanging around as ordered by Judge June."

"Sheriff, Sheriff, neigh, neigh," came

faint cries from the burlap sack.

Tuff asked Hooter, "Judge June told us you flew over to Lincoln County. What did you find out?"

"There are two good hiding places in Lincoln County – Saragosa Springs and Cloudcroft

Canyon. Sheriff Robin is in Cloudcroft Canyon, near Thunderhead Mountain. There's a stream around an island in a forest, almost like a castle with a moat. It's a good spot to hide."

GET UP!

"OK," said Tuff. "I have a plan which could work. Sawbones and I will join Crooked Jim's gang."

"What?" said Sawbones. "Are you crazy?"

"No, I'm not crazy, just listen to the plan." Tuff lowered his voice. "We disguise ourselves as a couple of outlaw cowboys from Texas. We ride into Lincoln County and ask for work with The Nasty Boys. Hopefully Crooked Jim will hire us. After we're in the gang, we tell them we know where Sheriff Robin is hiding out. But we tell them the wrong spot – Saragosa Springs. Crooked Jim is sure to take his outlaws and attack."

"I get it," Sawbones said. "That will delay them so the soldiers from Camp Beak can get to Sheriff Robin."

"Great plan, Tuff," Hooter said. "Now let's get you and Sawbones disguised as outlaw cowboys. I'll also disguise myself as a human and follow along on my horse, Speedy, in case I can be useful."

CHAPTER FOUR

COWBOYS LOOKING FOR WORK

Hooter grabbed a bucket of paints and brushes and went to work on Tuff's disguise. The owl turned Tuff's hair a muddy gray color and drew a scruffy beard around his mouth. A dirty black hat, red bandana, scuffed-up boots and chaps completed the outfit.

"Wow," said Sadie. "Dirtiest cowboy I ever saw."

"Here you go, Sawbones," Hooter said. He lathered buckets of filthy mud from the horse stables over Sawbones, painted dusty streaks through his curly black hair and drew skull and crossbones on his black eye patch.

"My, my," Sadie said. "Another filthy cowboy. EWW, what's that smell?"

"It's my newest smell for disguises." Hooter laughed as he splashed a disgusting mixture over the pretend cowboys. "Wild Thing's poop plus catfish guts mixed in a bucket of Mr. Zip's wee."

"Now we smell like outlaws," Tuff said as he almost gagged. "Let's ride."

Tuff and Sawbones headed into the stables and their horses came straight over to them. Tuff loved Silver Heels, his massive chestnut stallion. Sawbones rode Jack, a gray mustang. They hopped up on their horses and grabbed the reins.

"You guys really stink," Silver Heels whinnied.

Jack nodded in agreement. "You smell like outlaws."

"Good luck, cowboys," Sadie called to her brave friends as they rode out of the stables into Muleshoe's Main Street.

"Hold it, look there," Tuff said. "It's the singing cowboy poet."

The tiny cowboy sat in his usual spot on the veranda of the Happy Days Saloon. He kicked back in his rocking chair and sang:

Dressed like cowboys
Lookin' for cattle
But what they'll find
Is the biggest battle

Whispering Jesse
Versus Billy the Kid
Crooked Jim's boy
Won't like what he did

Watch out Tuff
Nothing seems to change
Bad guys against good
In a fight for the range

"Hey cowboy," Tuff called out. The elf disappeared.

"That song was scary," Sawbones said.

"We'll be alright," Tuff said. But his head spun with worry.

Tuff and Sawbones galloped toward the setting sun. "Lincoln County is due west of Muleshoe," Tuff said. "Let's ride till it's almost dark then bed down for the night."

The high plains were wet from the earlier thunderstorm. Dew glistened off small yellow and pink desert flowers that only bloomed after rain.

They soon passed a small wooden sign that hung off a barbed wire fence.

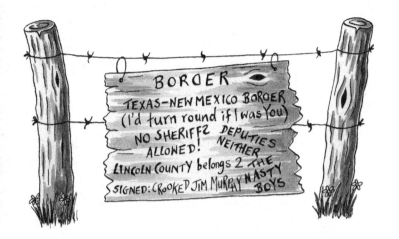

I'd turn around if I was you, Tuff thought. *I don't like that one little bit.*

"Want to turn back?" Sawbones asked.

"No," Tuff replied. "We've got a job to do."

They stopped their horses beside a small canyon. Red sandstone and pale limestone rocks surrounded a small campfire set under a clump of green mesquite trees.

"How about this place for the night?" Tuff said. "Looks like someone camped here before us."

He dismounted and bent down over the campfire. "The embers are still warm," he said. "I can smell smoke. They must have just gone."

"Good spot," Sawbones said. "I'll gather some dry wood and get the fire going."

"CLICK!" "CLICK!"

The unmistakeable sound of cocked Winchester rifles bit through the cool evening air. Sawbones stopped in his tracks.

"You fellas lost?" snarled a gruff voice from behind the trees. "Or maybe you cain't read?"

"Yeah, you shoulda turned around at the border. Lincoln County belongs to us," said another voice from the other side of the camp. "Put yer hands up."

Tuff looked at Sawbones as they raised their hands.

"We're not lost," Tuff said. "We're cowboys, looking for work. Who are you guys?"

"None of yore business," said an outlaw as he stepped from behind the trees. "But you coulda asked permission before you invaded our camp. How can two little kids be cowboys? Yore no bigger than fleas."

"We didn't know it was your camp," Tuff replied. "We would have ridden on if we knew. We may be small, but we can rope any old cow."

"Alright, then," the cowboy said, lowering his rifle. "Where you from? What are yore names?"

"I'm called Tuff. This is Sawbones. We're from Texas."

"You shore smell like Texans," sneered the other outlaw cowboy. "You boys can bed down tonight. We'll send you on your way in the mornin'. But you'll report to our boss. He'll want to lay eyes on ya both. I doubt he'll think you can do the job."

"Thanks," Sawbones said. "We're happy to report to your boss. We need work bad.

What's he called?"

"Our outfit's called The Nasty Boys. Boss is named James Murphy," said the cowboy. "Everybody calls him Crooked Jim. Best you call him 'sir'. He's nineteen. He carries two loaded Colt six-shooters and a bucketful of bad mood with him at all times."

Oh dear, thought Tuff. *I'm not sure joining the gang is such a good idea.*

CHAPTER FIVE

MY NAME'S CROOKED JIM

A swoop of migrating sandhill cranes woke Tuff the next morning. He heard the shrill bugle calls of the birds every spring as they flew north from Old Mexico to Canada.

"Sawbones, wake up," Tuff said as he shook the snoring doctor awake. "Looks like we're alone." The camp was empty except for Silver Heels and Jack.

Sawbones yawned as he shook the sleep out of his head.

They saddled up their steeds.

"Look, here come the two cowboys from last night," Sawbones said. "They've got somebody with them."

The two outlaws walked their horses along, leading another horse and its rider between them. Tuff recognized Hooter's bay colt, Speedy.

"Oh no," he whispered.

"Look what we found sneakin' around last night," said one outlaw. "A horse trader. Sez his name is 'Hooter'. Crooked Jim don't like traders one bit. He knows they're all thieves. So we're gonna see what he wants to do with him. You boys ride with us and make sure the thief doesn't try to escape. We're headed for town."

Hooter looked straight at Tuff. He slowly winked one eye.

We better make sure Hooter does escape, Tuff thought.

The two outlaws led the way. Soon they

were in the town. The walls of the burned-out buildings were pockmarked with bullet holes. Outlaws on horseback roamed the muddy streets, telling jokes then jumping in and out of fist fights.

"Man, this place is rough," said Sawbones.

There was an awful stench in the town. It smelled like horse poop mixed with mountain lion guts, left for two days under a hot sun.

We better help Hooter right now, Tuff thought. He leaned down right next to Speedy's ear. "Whoopee, we made it to town," he cried.

As Tuff hoped, Speedy reared back on his hind legs then took off like a cannonball. Out of town they flew, Hooter holding on with his short legs.

"Oops," Tuff said, "that horse must be scared of shouting cowboys. Want me to chase him down?"

"Naw, let him go," said the lead outlaw. "Let's go meet the boss. He should be at the saloon."

Tuff, Sawbones and the outlaws tied up their horses outside the Sour Grapes Saloon, a dirty wooden building with every window cracked or broken.

They pushed open the batwing doors and walked in to an almost empty room. "Well, whatcha got there, fellas? Did you bring me some tiny elves?" asked a high-pitched voice from the bar. "I bet it's a couple of stinky Texans."

The speaker was short with a round belly hanging over his green trousers. He had on a vest with two green feathers hanging down either side. Filthy red hair and a thick red beard hung over his ruddy face. His green bloodshot eyes stared at them from under a bright red bandana wrapped around his head.

"Howdy boys," he said. "My name's Crooked Jim. Who are you?"

"I'm Tuff. This is Sawbones. We want to work as cowboys."

"Work? That's for do-gooders," Crooked Jim said. "We don't work. We're outlaws. We steal from the rich, the poor and everybody in between. You kids are too little to be cowboys. Only help we need are lookouts for our gang. Same job as these two boys what brought you in here."

"If that's the only jobs you have, we'll take 'em," Tuff said.

"My gang's called The Nasty Boys. I'm havin' a bit of trouble right now with Sheriff Robin and his posse, The Bobbies. They're playin' a game of chickin', hidin' out somewhere. You can help me find 'em. There are only two good places to hide – Cloudcroft Canyon and Saragosa Springs. They have to be in one of those spots."

"We've got our own bullwhips," said Tuff.

"I can see that," said Crooked Jim. "You boys pretty fast with those? They're almost bigger'n you are."

"Fast enough," Tuff said.

"Good," said Crooked Jim. "Maybe I'll let you ride out front when we go after The Bobbies. You can be the first to take on Billy the Kid. He's workin' for 'em."

So Judge June was right, Tuff thought. *Oh dear, Billy the Kid.*

CHAPTER SIX

HENRY McCARTY, IT'S YOU

Crooked Jim pointed at a sleazy, filthy outlaw alone at the end of the bar.

"That there is 'Whispering' Jesse, my right-hand boy. Jesse's leadin' the hunt for Sheriff Robin. He'll be yore boss."

Whispering Jesse stared at Tuff. His black eyes were set in a face full of scars.

"He looks like somebody rubbed his face with a cactus," Sawbones whispered.

Jesse was thin, dressed in dirty black chaps and a vest. Two black six-shooters were in his holsters. Two sheathed Bowie knives hung from his belt. His boots had several small silver stars attached to them.

"I see yore lookin' at his boots," Crooked Jim said. "I give him a silver star every time he gets rid of an enemy of mine. He's never lost a gunfight."

"Follow me," Whispering Jesse said. Tuff could tell how he'd got his name.

Tuff and Sawbones followed the outlaw out of the Sour Grapes Saloon.

Whispering Jesse said, "Now listen up. We gotta find Sheriff Robin and his posse. Crooked Jim's never had anybody challenge him like The Bobbies. They need snuffin' out."

He mounted his black colt. The horse was scrawny with a mangy coat. As Tuff hopped up on Silver Heels, he felt his mount try to pull away from Whispering Jesse's colt.

Even the horses are nasty outlaws, he thought.

"We had some spies out. We heard The Bobbies might be hiding in Cloudcroft Canyon," Whispering Jesse said.

"Think so?" Tuff asked as he glanced toward Sawbones. "We ran into a couple of Navajo Tribe Indian Scouts on our way here. They said they saw a sheriff and a bunch of gunfighters gathered in Saragosa Springs. So there's no reason to go to Cloudcroft Canyon. The Bobbies won't be there."

"Saragosa Springs," said Whispering Jesse. "It's the other good place to hide. Let's ride over there and have a look."

Good, Tuff thought. *My plan is working. We'll stay away from Cloudcroft Canyon.*

The Rocky Mountains loomed in the distance as the trio galloped out of town. The air felt dry and clean. Tall green pine trees replaced the scraggly mesquite trees of the high plains.

"We don't know our way around New

Mexico," Sawbones whispered to Tuff. "Where are we?"

"I have no idea," Tuff said. *I hope this isn't a trap.*

"There's Thunderhead Mountain," Whispering Jesse said as they came around a small hill. "Cloudcroft Canyon's just below there."

"Didn't you say we were going to Saragosa Springs?" Tuff asked.

"Yep, I said that."

Whispering Jesse lowered his hand to his Colt. "But I never trust a stranger. When you told me to stay away from Cloudcroft Canyon I thought you were tryin' a trick."

Tuff saw Silver Heels' ears prick up. "BANG! BANG!"

"Get down, Sawbones," Tuff yelled. "Ambush."

Sawbones had already jumped to the ground and taken cover behind a large gray boulder.

Tuff hopped in next to him. "Whispering Jesse was shot." He pointed to the black-clad outlaw, slumped over in his saddle.

"Guess all those weapons didn't do him any good," Sawbones said.

"Your bull-whips won't do you any good, either," a voice behind them said. "Hands up. Now."

Tuff and Sawbones raised their hands in the air. "Now turn around, nice and slow," ordered the voice.

Tuff slowly turned. He was face to face with a short, skinny, blond-headed boy who had a nasty look in his sky-blue eyes. His two front teeth stuck out like a squirrel's.

"Henry McCarty," Tuff cried. "It's you."

CHAPTER SEVEN

SHERIFF ROBIN'S HIDEAWAY

"What?" Sawbones said. "That's Billy the Kid. What's got into you, Tuff? Don't make him mad."

"Henry's his real name," said Tuff. "We changed it to Billy on the way out West."

"Did he call you Tuff?" the famous gunfighter said in surprise. "Is that you, Tuff Brunson? From New York City?"

"It's me." Tuff smiled. "Sorry I look and smell like an outlaw, but I can explain that."

"You rode in with somebody from a vicious gang," said Billy, looking at Jesse with disgust. "But I know you'd never be an outlaw, Tuff."

"So you're the famous Billy the Kid," Tuff said. "You said you were coming to New Mexico Territory when we left Wichita. Looks like you got rid of your slingshot and use six-shooters now."

"Yup," Billy said. "Here, you can have my slingshot. You might need it sometime." Billy reached in his back pocket and pulled out the ebony-handled slingshot he brought from New York City. He handed it to Tuff. "I'm a gunfighter now. Who's your sidekick?"

"This is my deputy, Sawbones," Tuff said.

"Deputy? You're joking," Billy exclaimed.

"No, I'm not. I'm the Sheriff of Muleshoe, Texas and Sadie's a deputy too. We work for Judge June Beak."

"The magical judge?" Billy whistled. "So you're the sheriff with the fast bullwhip that everybody talks about? I heard Judge June sends Deputies out 'cause her magical power only works while she's in Muleshoe. If she leaves her town she's no longer a witch."

"I guess that's us," Tuff said. He tucked Billy's slingshot into his saddlebags. "How'd you know about Judge June?"

"I make it my business to know lots of stuff. It's how I survive as a gunfighter. C'mon, Tuff," Billy said. "Let's ride up and meet my boss and best friend, Sheriff Robin. You can tell us all about this outlaw racket you're messed up in."

Billy led the way up into Cloudcroft Canyon. Tuff noticed several sentries guarding the trail.

"Those must be The Bobbies," he said to Sawbones.

"Why is the posse called The Bobbies?" Sawbones asked Billy.

"'Cause Sheriff Robin comes from England. Over there all the law officers are called Bobbies."

The canyon was beautiful, with tall pines framing a small island surrounded by a swift blue stream. Several campfires sent up plumes of gray smoke.

The smell of barbequed bison filled the air, reminding Tuff he hadn't eaten breakfast.

"Hey, Sheriff Robin," said Billy. "Come look at who I found."

The tall sheriff appeared from behind a large boulder in the back of the camp. He was dressed neatly, with crisp trousers tucked into polished brown boots. A tan broad-brimmed hat shaded his smooth face above the blue bandana wrapped around his neck. His friendly eyes had a curious look.

"Who are these chaps? They're quite small to be wandering about," said Sheriff Robin. "I should say they also smell rather badly."

"I know they don't look like it, but this

is Sheriff Tuff Brunson and his deputy, Sawbones. They're from Muleshoe," Billy answered.

"Muleshoe? That's Judge June Beak's hideout kids town. My goodness, what in the world are you doing *here*, looking like that," Sheriff Robin exclaimed. "I've heard all about you, Sheriff Brunson. You're rather the hero, aren't you?"

"Nice to meet you," Tuff said. "Good to see my friend Billy as well."

Sheriff Robin's jaw dropped. "You two know each other?"

Billy grinned. "That's right. We were friends back in New York City. We came out West together but split up in Wichita. Tuff's the only boy to ever whup me. I haven't forgot that Tuff Brunson."

"Sorry about our appearance," Tuff said. "But I can explain it."

"Do sit down, let's have something to eat," Sheriff Robin said as he spread his arms out

over a huge meal of bison steaks, pheasant eggs and s'mores. "Tell me how you come to be here."

"We were sent by Judge June," Tuff explained as he munched on a steak. "She had a request for help from General Lew Wallace. Judge June sent her familiar, the owl Hooter, to find your hideaway and now General Wallace knows where you are he has sent US Army soldiers to protect you."

"That makes sense. But why are you dressed like outlaws?" Sheriff Robin asked.

"General Wallace needed time to get the Army here before Crooked Jim could find you. To trick Crooked Jim and delay him Sawbones and I disguised ourselves as outlaw cowboys and joined his gang," Tuff said. "We hope he'll believe us when we tell him you're hiding in Saragosa Springs, not here in Cloudcroft Canyon."

"Sounds like a great plan," Sheriff Robin said. "But you should hurry back to Crooked

Jim and tell him before he finds out we're not in Saragosa."

"We will. A warning though. Once they discover you're not in Saragosa Springs, they'll attack here right away," Tuff said as he and Sawbones put down their empty plates and jumped back on their horses. "Crooked Jim knows you are either in Saragosa or Cloudcroft."

"Not to worry," said Sheriff Robin. He was calm. "We'll be ready. Especially if the Army gets here in time."

"See you again soon," Tuff said to Billy as he and Sawbones galloped out of camp.

CHAPTER EIGHT

HOOTER SWOOPS IN

The two Deputies rode fast across the foothills.

Tuff slowed Silver Heels as they entered the town. "Something's strange," he said.

A massive gang of outlaws astride their horses lined the main street. They stared angrily at Tuff and Sawbones as they rode past. The outlaws fingered their Colts and rifles. Drawn knives shimmered in the sun.

As Tuff slowly rode toward the Sour Grapes Saloon he saw Crooked Jim sitting on a horse in front of it. Next to Crooked Jim stood Whispering Jesse's black colt.

Tuff's heart raced. Whispering Jesse sat on the ground beside his horse.

"You're back," hissed Crooked Jim. "In better shape than my right-hand boy who got all shot up. He was fine when he left with you. What happened to him?"

Tuff stared bravely at Crooked Jim. "We were ambushed by The Bobbies near Cloudcroft Canyon. Whispering Jesse was in front and was shot by Billy the Kid."

"Whispering Jesse didn't tell me he was goin' there. You must have taken him to Cloudcroft."

"We heard from Navajo Scouts that Sheriff Robin was in Saragosa Springs," Tuff said. "Whispering Jesse decided to go to Cloudcroft Canyon instead."

"NAVAJO SCOUTS?" Crooked Jim

screamed. "Stop lyin' and start truthin'. You're spies. STRING 'EM UP NASTY BOYS. HANG 'EM HIGH."

Hundreds of six-shooters were drawn. Tuff heard the clicks as he and Sawbones were forced toward huge wooden gallows that stood behind the saloon. "This could be it for us," Sawbones said.

Tuff stared straight ahead. "I'm not ready to say goodbye yet."

Two rope nooses were strung tight around Tuff and Sawbones' necks as they sat on their horses. The town became very quiet.

"Any last words, spies?" snarled Crooked Jim.

"Yeah, you ugly outlaw," Tuff answered, remembering Judge June. *Be afraid of nothing.* "Crime doesn't pay."

"WHOOOOSH!"

Hooter swooped down and bit through the two ropes. Silver Heels and Jack took off like the tornado wind, carrying Tuff and

Sawbones out of the town as outlaw bullets whistled by. Hooter flew along above them. "Glad I didn't miss," Hooter said as he bared his teeth. "Those ropes weren't easy to chew."

"I knew you'd watch out for us," Tuff said. "But Crooked Jim will attack Cloudcroft Canyon now. The Army won't have time to get there."

"Follow me. I made a small camp nearby. We'll get ready for the battle and rush over to Cloudcroft," Hooter said.

The owl led the way into a forest of Rio Grande Cottonwood trees. Disguised behind the trees was a campground and in the center of the campground was a familiar figure with ponytails.

"Sadie," Tuff exclaimed. "You're here."

"Sure am," Sadie said. "Judge June thought it was too important for me to stay in Muleshoe. I brought your sheriff outfit."

"Sadie, guess what? We met Billy the Kid and it turns out he's our old friend Henry McCarty."

"Really!" Sadie looked surprised. "You can tell me more later. But now let's get you and Sawbones cleaned up."

Hooter took Tuff and Sawbones to a nearby waterfall. They scrubbed up in the cold water. Soon they sparkled in their white shirts, tan trousers and knee-high boots. The last thing Tuff put on was his belt with the golden stars.

Hooter flew over to a perch near the campfire.

"Don't forget your badges," Sadie said as Tuff and Sawbones put on their white hats and hopped up on their horses.

"Let's ride," Tuff said.

Tuff, Sadie and Sawbones galloped out of the camp. Their silver badges glistened in the sunshine.

Hooter flew overhead. "I know a secret way into the canyon," he said. "Follow me."

Hooter led them across the foothills down Roadrunner Creek. As they passed Thunderhead Mountain they approached the rim of the canyon.

"The trail drops steeply, be careful," Hooter said.

"Wait," Sadie said. She pointed over the canyon's rim.

They looked out over Cloudcroft Canyon. A thunderous herd of outlaws galloped toward it.

"The Army is nowhere in sight," Tuff said. *We may be on our own against hundreds. How can we fight all of them? What if Judge June's magic doesn't work?*

CHAPTER NINE

THE BATTLE OF CLOUDCROFT CANYON

Led by Silver Heels, the Deputies' horses hurried down the steep hill. They crossed the stream surrounding Sheriff Robin's island camp.

"What the —?" Tuff exclaimed. "They're here."

Army soldiers filled the camp. Set around its perimeter were guns that Tuff had heard about but never seen before.

"Wow, Gatling Guns," Tuff said. "They look like single shot cannons but they can fire six shots very quickly."

"Welcome back, Sheriff Brunson," Sheriff Robin said. "I see you brought both your deputies. Billy's been telling me about Sadie. That's well and good because the General here wants Crooked Jim arrested."

"Hello, Sheriff Brunson," a tall, black-bearded gentleman said, extending his hand. "I'm General Lew Wallace, Governor of the New Mexico Territory. It's good to have met your friend Billy the Kid."

"Nice to meet you, sir," said Tuff. "I'm glad you're here."

"I came to fight against these gangs of savages. The United States was founded on the rule of law. The President wants these outlaws stopped, for good."

"BAM!" "BAM!" "BAM!"

"Battle stations, soldiers," cried General

Wallace. "The enemy are upon us."

Waves of filthy outlaws whooped and screamed as they galloped their horses toward the island. Bullets whistled overhead and thwacked into the pine trees.

"Fire at will," the General commanded.

A huge roar rose from the campsite as the disciplined Army troops battled the waves of outlaws.

Tuff glanced over at his friend Billy the Kid. *Same as always,* he thought. *Cool as ice.*

"Watch out, Billy," warned Sadie. An outlaw was behind Billy with a Bowie knife drawn, ready to stab.

"CRACK!"

"Look out you dirty outlaw, here comes Sheriff Tuff Brunson!" Tuff cried as his bullwhip lashed the knife right out of the outlaw's hand.

"Tie him up," Tuff shouted. Sadie grabbed some rope.

"BAM!"

"Oh no," Billy cried. "Sheriff Robin's been hurt."

The gentle sheriff slumped over. "I'll take care of him," Sawbones promised as he moved the sheriff to safety behind a boulder wall.

Tuff and Billy peered over the wall top. "Is the Sheriff OK?" Billy asked.

Sawbones cradled Sheriff Robin in his arms.

"Oh dear," Tuff said softly. "C'mon, Billy, let's get back in the fight."

"They've hurt my boss." Billy lost his cool. "I've had enough of these varmints."

He ran to one of the Gatling Guns.

"BAM! BAM! BAM! BAM! BAM! BAM!"

Outlaws dropped like bugs swatted from the sky.

"Hold your fire," General Wallace ordered. "The enemy are in retreat."

Peace settled over the campsite. The Nasty Boys were defeated.

A few outlaws struggled to get away. In the distance Tuff saw Crooked Jim limping along beside his horse.

"Come with me, Sadie; let's go get him."

Tuff leapt up on to Silver Heels and Sadie on to her black mare Jenny. They galloped toward Crooked Jim.

Sadie's whip lashed out and around the vicious outlaw, drawing his arms tightly to his chest. She loaded him across Jenny's back.

"Crime doesn't pay, you filthy outlaw," Sadie said as Crooked Jim's horse ran off. "You're under arrest."

Tuff and Sadie started back toward the canyon.

They heard a sad, crying voice. "It's Billy," Tuff said. "Let's hurry back."

CHAPTER TEN

WANTED BY THE UNITED STATES ARMY

As soon as they got back to the campsite Sadie dumped Crooked Jim on the ground. Army soldiers surrounded him. After dismounting, Tuff ran over behind the boulder wall.

Sawbones looked at Tuff. "Sheriff Robin's hurt bad," he said.

Billy sobbed softly as he sat next to Sheriff Robin, his head in his hands. "They hurt my boss."

Tuff knew how hard Billy's life had been. The injury to Sheriff Robin was terrible for him.

"I'll be OK," Sheriff Robin whispered to Billy. "But I need to get to a hospital right away."

Billy's face changed. The nasty look came into his blue eyes. "Every single one," he said. "Every outlaw that was here, I will find. I'll give them my own kind of justice. Starting right now."

He jumped on his horse.

"Wait, Billy," Tuff said. "You can't take the law into your own hands. Leave it to us. We'll track down all the outlaws."

"Tuff's right," General Wallace said. "The Lincoln County War is over. Today's battle changed everything. I'm very sorry Sheriff Robin was injured. But if you go after them yourself, I'm afraid we'll consider you an outlaw."

"You don't understand, General," Billy said. "I only know one kind of justice."

"Don't Billy," Tuff cried, but it was too late.

Billy the Kid had shoot in his eyes.

"BAM!"

He shot Crooked Jim.

"Ha, ha," he said. "Catch me if you can, General." Billy spurred his horse toward the Rocky Mountains.

Sawbones ran to Crooked Jim. "He'll be OK; it's not a serious wound," the young doctor said.

General Wallace turned toward Tuff.

"Even though Crooked Jim is a savage outlaw our job is to take him to justice, not hurt him. Tuff, I know Billy's your friend," he said, "but he is now an outlaw. Arrest him. He's wanted by the United States Army."

"Yes, sir," said Tuff. "Sawbones, ask an

Army doctor to look after Crooked Jim and come with us."

"This is terrible," Sadie said as they rode out to look for Billy. "We have to arrest our friend."

"I know," said Tuff. "But it's our job."

The Deputies didn't have far to ride.

"BAM!" a single shot rang out.

"That's a warning shot," Billy called. He was on his horse just above the rim of Cloudcroft Canyon. "Stop where you are."

Hooter flew up and said, "Tuff, he trusts you. Ask him to speak to you one-on-one. Offer him safe passage to Muleshoe. My hunch is that Judge June will treat him fairly. That's all he wants."

"I'll try," Tuff said. "But I'm not sure he'll believe me." He trotted Silver Heels toward Billy.

"Billy," Tuff called. "I'll come to you alone and drop my bullwhip on the ground. Will you do the same with your guns?"

"Yeah, c'mon." Billy dropped his Colts to the rocky ground.

Tuff dismounted, dropped his bullwhip and walked over to Billy.

"I won't let you arrest me," Billy said as Tuff got closer. "I don't care what the General says. The New Mexico Territory judge is an outlaw. He'll throw me in prison if he gets his hands on me."

"What if I give you safe passage back to Muleshoe?" Tuff replied. "Judge June is wise and kind. She'll listen to the whole story about how you helped win the range war. You'll be in jail, at least for a while. But I'm in charge of the jail."

"Can you really do that?" Billy asked.

"Yep," Tuff said. "You've always got in trouble. While you're in jail, you can stay out of trouble."

"Then I agree," Billy said. "I trust you, Tuff."

"Let's go tell General Wallace."

"Stop right there. Now," snarled a bloody outlaw as he stepped from behind a thick cactus. "Where are your guns, Billy the Kid, Mr. Genius of Shoot? Where's your bullwhip, Sheriff?"

Billy and Tuff froze in their tracks.

"You boys are sittin' ducks," the outlaw said as he raised his silver Colt. "Think I'll finish you both off."

Tuff took off his silver badge, carefully placing it in the palm of his hand.

If this works, Tuff thought, *then Judge June's magic is more powerful than I ever imagined. Please work!*

The outlaw pointed his gun straight at Billy's heart.

"Let's see if you bleed as fast as you shoot," he said.

"BAM!"

CHAPTER ELEVEN

THE ARREST OF BILLY THE KID

Billy took a sharp breath. "He missed me. How?"

"How did I miss him?" the outlaw said.

Tuff handed the outlaw's bullet to Billy. "He didn't miss. My badge got in the way," he said.

"CRACK!"

"Here comes Deputy Sadie."

"CRACK!"

"Here comes Deputy Sawbones."

The two deputies had snuck up behind the outlaw. Their whips lashed him, reining in his gun and dropping him to the ground.

"Tie him up," Tuff said. "Nice work, deputies."

"Whew," Billy whispered to Tuff. "What they say about you is true. You're magical. Nobody can catch a bullet in flight. But I just seen it happen."

"Billy, I know you won't like it but I have to handcuff you. I'll carry your guns," Tuff said. "You'll get them back when you get out of jail. I'll cuff your hands in front so you can ride your own horse."

"That's alright by me," Billy replied.

"OK, then," said Tuff as he slapped handcuffs on the scariest gunfighter in the Wild West. "Billy the Kid, you're under arrest."

Tuff picked up his bullwhip and Billy's six-shooters and hopped on Silver Heels. The others remounted their horses. "Quick stop to talk to General Wallace," Tuff said. "Then home to Texas."

They rode back into the canyon and slowed their horses as they crossed the stream on to the island. They found General Wallace writing on parchment in the shade of a big pine.

"We're back, General," Tuff said. "Are you writing about the battle?"

"No, I'm working on a book called *Ben Hur*. Looks like you captured the outlaw."

"We got him," Tuff said in a friendly voice. "He's under arrest."

"Good work, Sheriff Brunson. My troops will turn him over to the judge here in New Mexico."

"General Wallace, we've promised to take him to Muleshoe. We think he will be treated more fairly there."

General Wallace put down his pen and thought for a moment.

"That's fine with me," he said, "on one

condition. Please tell Judge June that, if he is released from jail, he is *not* to return to New Mexico Territory. He is an outlaw and my job is to clear the Territory of outlaws."

"You have my word," Tuff answered. "Billy?"

Billy just nodded. He said nothing.

"Then we'll get going. Goodbye General," Tuff said. "Let's ride."

The Deputies rode across the Texas border with their prisoner as Hooter fluttered above. "Not far to Muleshoe now," Sawbones said.

"I'm ready for a big plate of s'mores and a gallon of sarsaparilla," Sadie said. "Let's go straight to the Happy Days."

All of the hideout kids lined Main Street as Tuff led the Deputies and their prisoner into Muleshoe.

BILLY!

BILLY!

BILLY!

BILLY!

BILLY THE KID!

Hooter said, "I believe they want to see the world-famous gunfighter Billy the Kid."

Hooter was right. "Look this way, Billy," said Not-So-Fast Freddie. "Over here, Billy," hollered Howard the Coward.

"Did you bring me any mash, Billy?" growled Wild Thing. "Isn't a baby goat called a kid? Are you a goat? Ha, ha."

"Be quiet, Wild Thing," Wandering Wanda said. "Or you might have to eat a bullet one day."

"Welcome back," said Judge June as they rode up to the jailhouse. "I understand you have brought in a prisoner."

"We have," Tuff replied.

"You're a long way from New York City," Judge June said to Billy. "We will treat you fairly. Tuff, please put Billy in a jail cell. We'll call him to trial shortly."

"Thank you, Judge June," Billy said.

After Billy was locked up, Tuff asked, "Are the Parrots still in their burlap sack?"

Judge June laughed. "No, they're in a birdcage inside a jail cell. I've put a blanket over it so they can sleep. I'll decide what to do with them soon enough."

"Ha!" Tuff grinned. "Hope you have that cage locked up nice and tight."

"I do," Judge June said as she reached into her pocket. "Here you go. It's a special golden star for your belt, for bringing in Billy the Kid. Nice job, Sheriff. Let's go to the Happy Days Saloon everybody. S'mores and sarsaparilla on the house."

THE END

Author's Note

Each of the Hideout Kids series of books features several of the same characters, animals, places and things. Here are some brief descriptions:

Charlie "Sir" Ringo: A cowboy detective.

Deputy Joe "Sawbones" Newton: Muleshoe's doctor, a deputy to Sheriff Tuff Brunson.

Deputy Sadie Marcus: Ten-year-old deputy of Muleshoe and Tuff's best friend.

Hooter: Judge June's familiar. An owl-shaped spirit who helps Judge June practice her magic.

Jack: Sawbones' horse.

Jelly Roll Jim, Toothless Tom, Deputy Dan Pigeon: Teenagers who grew up in Muleshoe and stayed on to help Judge June and the hideout kids.

Jenny: Sadie's horse. A gift from Chief Ten Bears of the Comanche Tribe Indians.

Judge Junia "June" Beak: United States District Judge of the West. She is also a good and powerful witch.

Mesquite trees: Typical tree of the Texas desert.

Miss Hannah Humblebee: A Hopi Tribe Indian girl detective.

Mr. Zip: Tuff's pet. A beaver.

Muleshoe, Texas: Home of the hideout kids. Only children can find it and live there.

S'mores: Chocolate-covered marshmallows, served on sugar crackers. Dee-lish.

Sarsaparilla: The most popular soft drink of the Wild West. It's thought to have healing powers and is made from the root of the sarsaparilla vine. Yummy.

Sheriff Tuff Brunson: Ten-year-old sheriff of Muleshoe.

Silver Heels: Tuff's horse. Also a gift from Chief Ten Bears.

Spiky: A giant saguaro cactus that guards The Cave.

The Cave: A magical place where the kids can travel through time.

The Singing Cowboy Poet: A magical elf.

Wild Thing: Judge June's pet. A pink fairy armadillo.

Here are descriptions of a few animals, plants and things that you might not have seen before and which appear in this book:

Bed down: Climb into your bedroll and go to sleep.

Bowie knife: Named after the famous Jim Bowie, a long, sharp knife with a heavy handle.

Colt or Colt 45: The common pistol in the Wild West.

Dung beetles: A small beetle that loves to eat horse, cow and buffalo poop. Really!

Gatling Gun: The first Army gun able to fire several bullets very quickly.

Parchment: Paper in the old days.

Rio Grande Cottonwood trees: Tall trees of the New Mexico Territory.

Sandhill cranes: Beautiful gray birds with long swooping wings and a distinctive song, a "shrill". They migrate over 1,000 miles every spring and autumn, from north to south and back.

Winchester rifles: The common rifle in the Wild West, used mostly for shooting animals for food.

JUDGE ROY BEAN & WILD THING

Chapter One
BILLY THE KID IS GUILTY

It was a late spring afternoon in the Wild West town of Muleshoe. The setting sun shone brightly in the pretty blue sky. A group of happy hideout kids played a game of football on Main Street.

They didn't have a real football so they used a big ball of dried-up buffalo poop, tightly wrapped in long pampas grass.

Sheriff Tuff Brunson left the Muleshoe jail and led a prisoner across the street. The prisoner was Billy the Kid, the most famous outlaw in the Wild West. Billy's wrists were handcuffed. He shuffled along in his leg irons. His head hung down and his eyes stared at the ground.

"Phew, what's that smell?" Tuff asked as he passed the kids. "It smells worse around here than it ever has."

"Our football. It kind of stinks every time you kick it," laughed Wandering Wanda. Wild Thing ran up and punched the ball with her nose. "I think it smells great," the pink fairy armadillo growled. "Just like my mash."

I know the football smells bad, Tuff thought, *but something else smells terrible. I wonder what it is?*

Wanda asked Tuff, "Hey, where are you going with your ugly prisoner, Billy the Kid? He doesn't look so scary since you arrested him in New Mexico and locked him up in the jail. Want to play football, Billy?" Wanda kicked the ball right at Billy's head, which snapped back as the poop splattered around his ears. "Oops," she laughed.

Wild Thing howled with laughter. "Good shot, girlfriend," she said to her favorite hideout kid. Billy glared at Wanda and whispered under his breath, "I'll get you fer that."

"How's that, smelly?" Wanda laughed. "You're all locked up."

"Stop it, Wanda," Tuff said. "I'm taking Billy in to Judge June. It's time for his trial for shooting Crooked Jim."

Tuff took out his bandana, wiped the poop from Billy's head, then led his prisoner into the hut of the good witch and United States District Judge of the West, Junia "June" Beak. Tuff's best friend Deputy Sadie Marcus joined them inside the front door. Wild Thing tagged along.

Judge June waited at her desk. Tuff and Sadie led Billy to a spot in front of the witch. *I hope she's fair to him*, Tuff thought, *he is my old friend after all.*

"I find you guilty," said Judge June as she stared hard at Billy the Kid. "For your crime, I sentence you to spend the rest of your life in jail. The US Army is going to keep you in their prison. I want you locked up and the key thrown to the bottom of the ocean."

"But Judge June, you told me you would be fair," Billy cried. "You know I was tryin' to help Sheriff Robin and The Bobbies fight off the outlaw gang The Nasty Boys. I only shot Crooked Jim 'cause he shot Sheriff Robin."

"Judge June, that seems unfair. Billy is our friend," Sadie said.

"Yeah, he is but he broke the law," Tuff reminded Sadie. "Right after I warned him to stop."

"I am fair. Billy, you took the law into your own hands," Judge June said with a stern voice. "You shot an unarmed man as he lay on the ground. You're not fit to live among good kids. But if you'll promise to behave yourself in jail I'll see that you get out early."

"Behave?" Billy said. "I'd rather eat cockroaches."

"Me too," said Wild Thing.

Judge June looked at Billy. "Fine, you had your chance. Tuff, hand this prisoner over to the Army troops at Camp Beak tomorrow morning," she ordered.

Tuff and Sadie grabbed their old friend from New York City. Billy's arms strained at the handcuffs and he kicked hard, jangling his leg irons, as they forced him out of the hut.

"No!" Billy screamed. "This ain't fair."

The children stopped their game and ran over to watch as Tuff and Sadie crossed the street with their prisoner. "Want another splash of buffalo poop, kiddo?" Wanda said.

"Enough Wanda," Tuff said as they walked into the Muleshoe jail.

He turned toward his old friend. "I'm very sorry, Billy, but Judge June was fair. She offered you a chance to shorten your punishment," Tuff said. "You'll have to stay here one more night. We'll take you to Camp Beak in the morning."

Tuff and Sadie took off Billy's handcuffs and leg irons, put him back in his cell and locked the door.

Sadie turned up her nose. "What's that smell?" she asked. "It really stinks in here."

"I don't know," Tuff answered. "Actually I can't smell it now but there was a really horrible stench earlier. It seems to come and go."

Billy's face was a bright crimson red as he looked at Tuff. His voice was a low growl, like a mad bear's, as he said, "You'll never hand me over to the Army. I'll be long gone in the mornin'. And one more thing. You and me and Sadie might have been friends once. From now on we are sworn enemies. You better watch your backs."

"Sorry Billy but you're wrong about that. You can't escape. Sadie and I will stay here all night," Tuff said. "We've also got Deputy Sawbones to guard the outside."

"Not only am I leavin', I'm takin' The Parrot Gang with me." Billy scowled.

Sadie laughed. "The Parrot Gang? You mean the miniature Parrots and their little horses? I guess they're still in their birdcage in the next jail cell. Hey Parrots, are y'all still having a nap?"

"Let us out, let us out," the Parrots squealed in their weak baby voices. "Neigh, neigh," squeaked the tiny horses.

"Ever since they were shrunk by that lightning strike, that's all they've been able to say." Tuff smiled at Sadie. "'Big Nose' George, 'Little Nose' George and 'Tiny Nose' Peggy Parrot are no longer the meanest outlaws in the Wild West. But they're definitely the smallest."

"You cain't keep me in here, Tuff," Billy

said. "And guess what? I got a surprise for you. I think I'll also take Judge June with me when I leave Muleshoe. She won't have her magical powers when I get her out of this town."

"Now you're just crazy," Tuff said. But as he spoke, he felt a sudden breeze blow over him. "Sadie, what is it?" Tuff asked. "That awful smell has come around again." His head started to spin as he watched Sadie collapse to the dusty wooden floor. Her eyes were tightly closed. He looked outside and saw Sawbones fall to the ground, fast asleep.

What's happening to us? Tuff thought as his knees buckled and he fell to the floor. *I'm going to sleep. I must keep my eyes open. Oh dear...*

A huge black cloud blocked the evening sun. Darkness covered the little town.

So far in the HIDEOUT KIDS series...

MIKE GLEASON
HIDEOUT KIDS
TUFF, SADIE
& THE WILD WEST

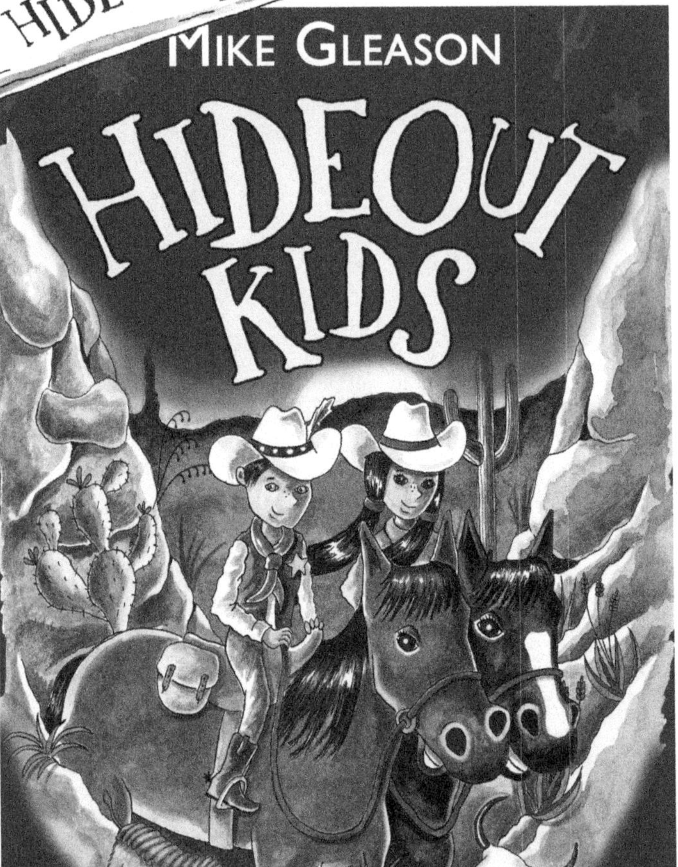

MIKE GLEASON

HIDEOUT KIDS

GENERAL MUSTER
& NO-TREES TOWN

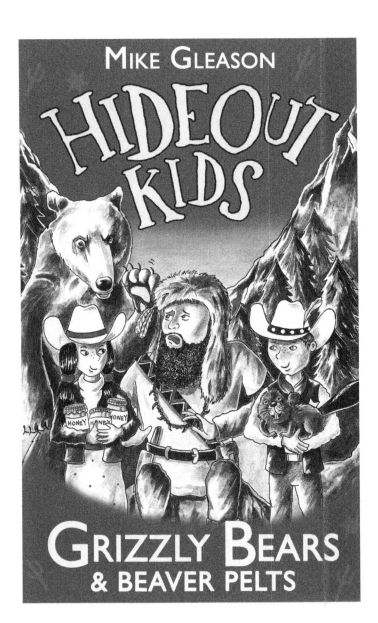

MIKE GLEASON

HIDEOUT KIDS

MACHO NACHO
& THE COWBOY BATTLE

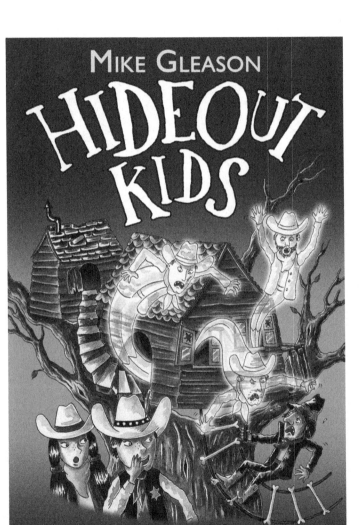

MIKE GLEASON

HIDEOUT KIDS

THE PARROT GANG
& WILD WEST GHOSTS

MIKE GLEASON

HIDEOUT KIDS

BILLY THE KID
& CROOKED JIM

MR. ZIP

WILD THING

JUDGE JUNE

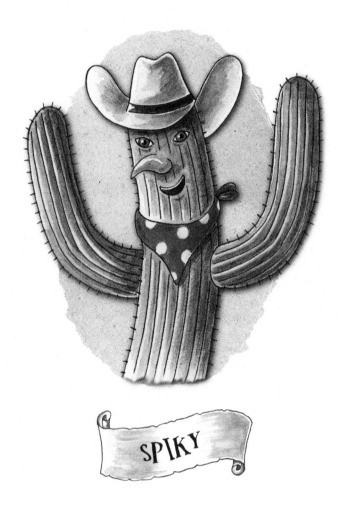

SPIKY

ABOUT THE AUTHOR

Hideout Kids author Mike Gleason comes from a small town in Texas. He grew up with cowboys, cowgirls and exciting stories of Wild West adventures. He was a wildcatter in the Texas oil fields and a board director at MGM in Hollywood. He created and produced an award-winning music television series at Abbey Road Studios. He lives and writes in London.

ABOUT THE ILLUSTRATOR

Hideout Kids illustrator Victoria Taylor comes from Cheltenham, England, and her love of art was inspired by her maternal grandmother. She trained at Plymouth University and worked for many years as a graphic designer. Having returned to her first love of painting and drawing, Victoria is now a freelance book illustrator. She lives in Gloucestershire with her husband and two children.

Made in the USA
Las Vegas, NV
07 January 2023

65217189R00072